DIA MINECRAFT ZOMBIE

BOOK 17

ZOMBIE'S eXCELLENT AdVENTURE

Koala Books
An imprint of Scholastic Australia Pty Limited
PO Box 579 Gosford NSW 2250
ABN 11 000 614 577
www.scholastic.com.au

Part of the Scholastic Group
Sydney • Auckland • New York • Toronto • London • Mexico City
New Delhi • Hong Kong • Buenos Aires • Puerto Rico

Published by Scholastic Australia in 2018.
Text copyright © Zack Zombie Publishing 2018.

All rights reserved. No part of this publication may be reproduced or transmitted in any form or by any means, electronic or mechanical, including photocopying, recording, storage in an information retrieval system, or otherwise, without the prior written permission of the publisher, unless specifically permitted under the Australian Copyright Act 1968 as amended.

This unofficial novel is an original work of fan fiction which is not sanctioned nor approved by the makers of Minecraft. Minecraft is a registered trademark of, and owned by, Mojang Synergies AB, and its respective owners, which do not sponsor, authorize, or endorse this book. All characters, names, places, and other aspects of the game described herein are trademarked and owned by their respective owners. Minecraft®/TM & © 2009-2018 Mojang.

NATIONAL LIBRARY OF AUSTRALIA

A catalogue record for this book is available from the National Library of Australia

ISBN 978-1-74276-868-7

Typeset in Agent 'C', Potato Cut TT and Bender.

Printed by Griffin Press, Salisbury South, SA.

Scholastic Australia's policy, in association with Griffin Press, is to use papers that are renewable and made efficiently from wood grown in responsibly managed forests, so as to minimise its environmental footprint.

18 19 20 21 22 / 1

DIARY OF A MINECRAFT ZOMBIE

BOOK 17

ZOMBIE'S EXCELLENT ADVENTURE

BY

Zack Zombie

SUNDAY

Pew! Pew! Pew!

'Take that!'

'Whoa! Are you just gonna let him do that to you?!!' asked Slimey, looking on as Skelee and I battled for our lives.

'No way! It's time to pull out my **SECRET WEAPON!**'

The game was gonna be over once I pulled out my Proton-Laser.

ZZZZZTT!

'Whoa!'

Or so I thought... suddenly, there was a pulsating ball of light as it was hurled in the air...

SSSHHHUUPPP!!! BOOMMM!!!

'Dude, you just got wiped out!' commented Creepy.

'Hey, no fair! you had the **PLASMA GRENADE!**'

'Sorry, bro, you gotta do what you gotta do,' Skelee said with a smug look on his bony face.

Man, that's the last time I play with these guys.

'Dude, this game is awesome! **CRAFTFORMERS** is so cool, right, Zombie?' Skelee asked.

I grunted in reply.

'You know what would be really awesome? If we combined and became our own Craftformer,' Creepy said. 'All our abilities will be combined, too!'

'Yeah, we'd be called **ULTIMUS**

SUPREME,' Skelee said.

Ultimus
Supreme

'What do you think, Zombie?'
Creepy asked me.

'Yeah... whatever.'

KLANG! KLANG! KLANG!

We were all interrupted by a loud banging noise coming from Steve's garage. But there's always noise at Steve's house.

Last time I slept over, I woke up and the house was shaking. But it was only Steve punching the side of his treehouse again.

I still don't understand the **PUNCHING TREE** thing. Especially since Steve's arms look like cankles.

KLANG! KLANG! KLANG!

We all walked over to the garage

where Steve was working.

'Steve, whatcha doing, man?' I
asked him.

'Well, I'm almost finished putting
the finishing touches on my Time
Travel Portal,' Steve said.

'Whoa! No way! Does it really
work?!!!' asked Slimey.

'There's only one way to tell,'
Steve said with his **MAD
SCIENTIST** grin.

'Oh, no way!' Skelee said. 'Last
time we tried your experimental

Portal, I ended up with three heads. People were making Wither jokes for weeks.'

'Hey, what happened to that **OTHER PORTAL** you made, Steve?' I asked him.

'It's over there,' Steve said, pointing to what looked like a broken Nether Portal. 'I worked out some of the kinks, but I can't get it to stop combining whatever goes through it.'

Then, suddenly, Creepy got a weird look on his face.

We all knew where this was going. There was no way Creepy was going to get us to do it.

That is... until **HE DARED US.**

Man, why do we do anything once it's a dare? It's like the call of the wild. You know, we lose all common sense and want to do something really dumb.

So, of course, we had to try Creepy's Craftformer idea.

'AUTO-MOBS, TRANSFORM!'

Then we all jumped head-first into

Steve's test Nether Portal...

FFFZZZZZZZSSSH!

MONDAY

Stayed home from school today.

Creepy's dare... not one of our better ideas.

The new mob around the block.

But at least now I'm really good with a **BOW AND ARROW.**

And I bounce every time I walk, which is kinda cool.

And I have a **REAL URGE** to punch a tree.

But for some reason I keep farting everywhere... like real bad.

HSSSSSSSS.

I can get used to being like this.

TUESDAY

All I can say is that I am never going to take a dare ever again.

The **GOOD NEWS** is that the effects wore off, and we're back to normal.

The bad news is that I'm still farting everywhere... like a lot.

HSSSSSSSS.

And one of my legs still bounces when I walk. And I thought I had a real bad limp before.

Now, I can't stop hitting myself in the face. But it did come in handy the other day when I wanted to get out of gym class. The teacher just gave me a look and sent me to the nurse's office.

Anyway, today Ms. Bones, told us to write an essay on what we want to be when we **GROW UP.** I knew exactly what I was gonna write about.

I'm going to write about the dream I've had ever since I found out where Zombies really come from.

And, no, Zombies didn't come from a secret military experiment gone wrong. And we didn't come from eggs, either. Turns out we were born when a game developer named **NOTCH** thought we'd be a great addition to Minecraft.

And he made like, a kazillion dollars.

So, after I learned the truth, my dream was to one day become a game developer like my hero, Notch. And someday, I'm gonna

make my own world-changing
game like Minecraft... and make a
KAZILLION DOLLARS.

I'd probably call my game
something like, Dwarf Fortress...
Dungeon Keeper... or even better,
ZombieCraft.

Something cool like that.

'Well, can anyone share what they
wrote for their essay today?' Ms
Bones asked the class.

'I want to be a Parkour Specialist,'
Skelee said.

'I want to be a personal trainer,'
Slimey said.

'Well, when I grow up, I want to
be a stuntman,' Creepy said.

The class was silent. No-one had
the heart to tell him.

'Well, I want to be a software
game developer like Notch,' I said.

GASP!

Suddenly, Skeleton and Zombie
kids' jaws dropped everywhere.
Then, the room went quiet.

'Uh... Zombie, unfortunately, it's against the law for mobs to be software game developers,' Ms Bones said. 'Only Humans can.'

It felt like Ms Bones just ripped my head off, jumped down my throat and stepped on my heart... which happened when I was a baby Zombie trying to ride a Chicken.

Anyway, my dream was crushed.

So much for the most amazing, interactive, **FIRST PERSON SANDBOX** game to exist.

And so much for my kazillions...

WEDNESDAY

I went to visit Steve at his house today to ask him about why only Humans could make video games.

'Hey, Zombie, what's cookin'?'

'Me, I guess? It happens all the time in summer. But, don't worry, you'll get used to the smell.'

 Anyway, what's on your mind?' Steve asked.

'Uh... how come only Humans are allowed to make video games? Like, I really want to make cool games like Notch and...'

'SHHHHHH!' Steve hushed as he placed his fingers over his lips. Then he pointed to his garage.

So we sneaked over to his garage, and he turned on the music real loud.

Then he whispered in my ear, 'Dude, they can hear you...'

'Wait, who can hear me?'

'The players, man...' Steve said again, pointing with his fingers in the air.

'What players?' I asked, getting a little worried about Steve.

'Dude... the Minecraft players.'

I still didn't know what in the world Steve was talking about.

'The **H–U–M–A–N** Minecraft players. They can hear what you're saying. And if they heard you talking about wanting to make video games, you could get in some real trouble.'

'Wait a minute. You mean, right now, there are Humans that can see everything we're doing and hear everything we are saying?'

'Yup.'

'Even when I got a really bad **EXPLOSIVE DIARRHOEA** and I tried keeping it in by taping my butt cheeks together... but it came out anyway... through my ear holes. And you're telling me they saw all that?'

'Uh huh.'

Suddenly, it all made sense. I

always felt like my life was one big **REALITY SHOW.** And I always had this feeling that somebody was watching me and even controlling me sometimes.

Like, that one time I smacked Jimmy the Creeper on the back of the head on a dare, I felt like something had totally taken control over me.

Anyway, this is crazy!

'So, dude, how come it's against the law for mobs to be game developers?' I whispered to Steve.

'It happened a few years ago, when MM Co. took over Mojang. Since then, they closed all the Minecraft Development schools and fired all mob game developers. Then they passed a law saying that **ONLY HUMANS** can make games.'

'And nobody did anything?!!'

'There wasn't much we could do. Once Notch sold out to MM Co., they took over everything. Now Humans control everything. Our only hope we have now is the prophecy.'

'Wait, what **PROPHECY?**'

'Well, they say that one day, one will be born in Minecraft that will come and free us from the control of MM Co. They call them... the Chosen One. No-one knows who he or she is. I mean, it could be you.'

Man, I've never been chosen for anything before.

Like, when we play basketball in gym class, nobody ever picks me to be on their team. I think it's because I run like a hundred-year-old man...

Or maybe it's because when I sweat, whatever (or whoever) my sweat lands on grows a new species of fungus. So, I always end up sitting on the mouldy bench... with the other **MOULDY NOOBS.**

But, man, could I really be like the Chosen One?

THURSDAY

Today we went on a field trip to the Minecraft History Museum.

It was awesome! I learned about all the updates that happened since Minecraft first started.

Fun fact: Minecraft used to be called the **CAVE GAME!**

I learned about Minecraft Update 1.5, where they first introduced Redstone into Minecraft. How did mobs get along without any

Redstone? How did they power their **ZPHONES?**

Then there was the Minecraft Update 1.7.10, which was when mods took over the world. It was like the Wild West of Minecraft!

I remember it, too. There was a mod for everything. There was even a mod I tried once called the X-ray mod. The guys and I had so much fun with it. We could see everything.

Anyway, the world got really crazy with Minecraft 1.7.10, so they had to shut it down.

And then... the ultimate Minecraft Update arrived...

Duh, duh, dun! Minecraft Update 1.8!

That was the most awesome update ever! Why?

Because it was all about the ADVENTURE, man... but then, after that, everything changed.

MM Co. came in and took over the Overworld. It was never the same again with the introduction of...

Duh, duh, dun! Minecraft Update 1.9!

It was downhill from that update on. PVP will never EVER be the same again. That **'COOL DOWN'** feature...

So wrong.

Anyway, at the end of the field trip, I saw an exhibit that talked about my hero, Notch. They said he was a pioneer.

In the beginning, he was all about the game. But then, something happened and he sold out... and left us mobs to face the **MM CO. ALONE.**

Wow, that took a down turn.

FRIDAY

Urrrrgggghhh! I'm so mad!

My mum and dad went to a parent-teacher conference yesterday and the topic was, 'Why Too Much Screen is Eating Away at Your Child's Brain'.

Since a Zombie's brain is about the **SIZE OF A PEA,** my parents got all crazy about it. I couldn't lose the little that I had left.

So, the first thing they did was

take away all my fun. They took my TV, laptop, gaming console, Pocket Console, zPad and zPhone. It was **TRAUMATISING.**

But, now that I've spent some time away, my parents might have a point. It was kinda weird that my thumbs were stuck in the same position for like a week.

But now, I don't even know what to do with myself.

Well, I guess I can organise my super-messy underwear drawer... I don't get what all the fuss is about underwear. Steve said he has seven pairs of underwear. One for each day of the week.

Me? I have twelve. One for January, February...

Anyway... what's a kid supposed to do with all this screen-less time? It's never-ending torture.

Mum said that I should read a **BUICK** to pass the time.

Or did she call it a **BLOOK?**

Whatever. I've heard that the graphics are terrible.

 SATURDAY

Well, my SCREEN DETOX didn't last long.

I think it was probably because the insurance company told my parents they wouldn't cover the damage. Not my fault that the experiment in my room just did not work...

Anyway, since my room was unliveable for a few days, the guys and I decided to sleep over at

Steve's house again.

My mum still thinks Villagers are weird and they smell funny.

But she likes Steve. I think it's because of his **SQUARE HEAD.**

Well, when we got to Steve's house, we started playing Craftformers. But after losing a few rounds to the guys, I decided to find Steve.

As I started walking to the backyard, all of a sudden...

FFFZZZZZZZSSSH!

'Hey, Steve! You okay?' I called out.

'EUUUREEEKKAA! Dude, I finally did it!' Steve yelled.

When I got there, there was a huge Portal that looked like it was made out of **DIAMONDS.**

Steve's new Portal

'What in the world is that?'

'It's my Time Travel Portal! And it's finally working! I'll prove it to you.'

Suddenly, Steve jumped into the Time Portal.

FFFZZZZZZZSSSH!

There's like no way that thing works. I mean, if time travel was possible, everybody would be doing it, especially on **ZTUBE.** That is... unless somebody went back in time and erased all the zTube videos about time travel.

Ugh... my head hurts.

But if it really did work, I would go back in time and fix all my embarrassing PRETEEN moments...

Like... 99% of my life that totally defines my existence.

I kept thinking about things I would want to fix and suddenly, Steve jumped back out of the Portal.

FFFZZZZZZZZSSSH!

'See, I told you it would work,'

Steve said with a very smug look on his face.

'What are you talking about?'

Then Steve pointed his fat finger at my shirt. I looked down.

'What the what?!!' There... on my shirt, in big green letters:

I'M A NOOB.

'I just jumped back in time a few minutes and wrote that on your shirt,' Steve said. 'It was hard to convince you... until I sweetened the offer with some cake.'

Then I looked in the mirror, and I still had icing on my face.

'Whoa! Dude, that's crazy!'

'Awesome, right? So, wanna take it out for a spin? We could play some **PRACTICAL JOKES** on the guys,' smirked Steve.

Man, it sounded really tempting.

But we probably shouldn't be messing with the fabric of the universe . . .

What if we mess up history? Or create a chain of events

that causes the destruction of Minecraft?

'Yeah, **I'M IN!**'

SUNDAY

FFFZZZZZZZSSSH!

We got back from our time travel
shenanigans really late.

Steve and I were so tired, we
didn't even have enough energy
to go out and see if our awesome
PRANKS worked.

So we pulled out our sleeping bags
and crashed in Steve's backyard
under the stars.

But you know, today was so much fun. I can't wait till tomorrow to see **WHAT HAPPENED** with our pranks!

MONDAY

Lick, Lick, Lick.

'WHAT THE WHAT?!!'

I was woken up this morning by a **RAINBOW SHEEP** licking my face.

'You boys want some breakfast?' the rainbow Sheep said.

What is that?

'Uh... yeah, sure,' Steve said, a bit freaked out.

Then another rainbow Sheep came out.

'Are you boys heading into town today? Baaaahhhhh!'

'What in the overworld is going on?' I whispered to Steve.

'I don't know. But we better just **PLAY ALONG** and find a way out of here,' Steve said and then turned to the rainbow Sheep. 'Um, yes sir. We're going into town.'

'Steve, are you okay? Have you been hitting those trees too hard?' the rainbow Sheep-man asked.

We were too freaked out to reply, so Steve and I snuck out of his house and **ESCAPED.**

'So... WHAT IS GOING ON?!!'

'Dude, don't ask me. I'm just as creeped out as you are,' Steve said. 'And where are the Villagers I stayed with... Owen and Emma?'

'Uh, bro... I don't know how to tell you this. But I think that was Owen and Emma,' I replied.

While trying to figure out what was going on, it started raining gumdrops.

Steve picked one up in his hand and looked at it. He threw it in his mouth and then had a big smile.

'Dude, it's like my favourite flavour. Watermelon.'

'Eww! Mummy, that strange boy with the box head ate **BIRD POOPIE,**' said a young Enderman.

'Let's go, dear. Those boys obviously don't have any manners,' the lady

Enderman said with her chin up in the air.

ENDERMEN HAD CHINS?!

Anyway, we looked up and right above us were a bunch of pink and yellow birds swirling around, dropping gumdrops on top of us.

But what can I say... they were watermelon flavoured. We really couldn't help ourselves.

MONDAY
LATER THAT DAY

We decided to go back to my village. As we walked back, everybody kept giving us weird looks. Especially me.

'What's up with these guys?' I whispered to Steve. 'It's like they'd never seen a Zombie before.'

But then we noticed there were only Villagers, Endermen and a whole lot of rainbow Sheep and other **PASSIVE MOBS,** like Chickens and Cows.

There wasn't a Zombie, Skeleton, Creeper or Slime anywhere.

I tried waving at them, but the Endermen just teleported out of there, the Villagers ran into their houses and the passive mobs just ran into the bushes.

'What the...?'

We hurried along and we finally made it to my house. I was really hungry so I went straight to the fridge. Sitting right there was a **HUGE CAKE!**

I buried my face into the cake,

when all of a sudden...

BBBAAAAAHHHHH!!!!!

'Who are you and what are you doing in my house?!' the crazy-looking rainbow Sheep said.

'What? I live here!'

'You do not! My husband, my two sons and I live here. That cake was for my son Wesley's 5th birthday party!'

'Wait a minute... Wesley?'

'Yes. What about my younger

son's name?' seethed the rainbow Sheep.

'Uh... your name wouldn't happen to be Mildred Beatrice Zombie, would it?'

'BAAAH! No, my name is Mildred Beatrice **SHEEPERSTON**, not Zombie. Now get out of my house!'

'Sheeperston?'

But before I could ask more questions, she got into position to sheep-kick me in the face. Steve and I were out the door before she could get the chance.

'You and your funny friend with the weirdly-shaped head better get out of here!'

SLAM!

'Dude! What just happened?' I asked Steve.

'Uh... I think we both know, dude.'

'You mean... that rainbow Sheep was... my mum? Which means that our time travelling pranks somehow backfired. And we ripped the **FABRIC OF THE UNIVERSE** so badly that the world we knew has been changed forever.'

'Uh... yeah, something like that.'

Then we just looked each other.

'WWWAAAAHHH!!!'

Normally, I could rely on Steve to **CALM ME DOWN** but this time, Steve was crying too.

TUESDAY

We woke up to the sound of sirens outside the cave we slept in.

'Dude, what's that?' I asked, still groggy from sleep.

Next thing we knew, a group of scary looking robots surrounded us, grabbed us and put **HANDCUFFS** on us.

BLEEP. BLEEP.

'What gives, man?!!!' Steve shouted.

Then they put bags over our heads and before we knew it, they threw us in a van.

SLAM!!!

Next time we saw light, we were tied to a chair in a **STRANGE ROOM.**

'You thought you could get away with it, didn't you?' a creepy sounding lady said.

'Mmmfff mmfffggrrmmff.'

'Take their hoods off!'

'I said, I really had to go do number two... but it's okay now,' I said as I got comfortable in my chair.

Blech! **SPLAT!**

'Who are you?' I asked the cold, but familiar-looking Human lady.

'You don't remember me? Maybe this will jog your memory...' she said as she undid the bun in her hair and took off her glasses and then shouted, 'ONE DAY, MINECRAFT WILL BE PARENT-FRIENDLY! I PROMISE YOU!'

'NO WAY!' Steve and I gasped.

'Yes it is I, Mabel Mumbottom! Also known as **MUMMA MABEL,** the CEO of MM Co.'

'WHAT?!!'

'I promised you my revenge. So I created my own Time Portal and travelled back 30 years and got a job at MM Co. as a cleaner. Then I spent those 30 years working my way up the ladder, plotting my revenge until I became CEO.'

Steve and I looked at each other in shock. Also... wow, her Time Portal could go back that far.

'And the first thing I did as CEO was to buy Mojang to gain total control of Minecraft. And once I got control of Mojang, I made it so that only Humans could be game developers.'

'That was you?!!!' Steve said.

'Yes. And then finalised my vision of Minecraft. I introduced in the Minecraft Update 1.9, which introduced the Cool Down effect, eliminating all the fun in PVP.'

'That was you too?!!!' Steve yelled.

'Yes, then after a series of parent-friendly updates, it would culminate to finally releasing the ultimate Mum Friendly Minecraft Update called...'

Then the robots next to Mabel got in formation and yelled, 'DUH, DUH, DUUNNN! **THE INFINITY UPDATE 2.0!**'

'We're going to stop you before that happens,' I said.

'But don't you see? The Infinity Update 2.0 is now! It got rid of every hostile mob and turned them into passive... rainbow Sheep!'

'OH NOOOOO!'

'MUAHAHAHAHA!' Mabel cackled like a Forest Biome swamp Witch.

This is crazy. That means everyone I know in my village has turned into rainbow Sheep!

'Hey, but what about Owen and Emma at my house?' Steve said. 'They were Villagers, they didn't hurt anybody!'

'Well, I heard about that 'Chosen One' prophecy, and I didn't want to take any chances. So I commanded Mojang to turn everybody in the Chosen One's village into Sheep too. I wouldn't want to wake up and find out the **CHOSEN ONE** ruined everything.'

Wait a minute! Then that means that Steve is the...!

'But, enough chit chat. My robot minions will take you to the special machine we call the **SHEEPINATOR!** It'll cure you

of all your troublemaking,' Mabel
continued. 'Then you two can
live quiet lives in your precious
Minecraft... or should I say...
MUM-CRAFT?'

'WHAT?!!! NOOOOOOO!' Steve and
I yelled as they dragged us away
to get Sheepinised.

TUESDAY
LATER THAT DAY

They threw us in a cell to wait
while they got the Sheepinator up
and running.

'Dude, we have to find a way
outta here,' Steve said.

'Yeah, but then what do we
do? Minecraft has been
transformed into an age-
appropriate experience, full of
**POSITIVE EDUCATIONAL
CONTENT...** it's terrible!'

'If we can go back to my house, we can use the Time Portal and try to fix this,' Steve said.

'**GOOD IDEA.** And I'm so glad that the "tearing the fabric of the universe" thing wasn't our fault. But how can we go back that far? We've never done it before...'

'Well, with a little tweaking, we can at least go back far enough to stop the Infinity 2.0 Update. She said it happened recently, right? Whaddya say, dude?'

'Let's do this!'

The good thing is that the cells weren't built for holding Zombies.

So, a little pull here and a little snap there, I was able to slip through the cell bars.

Once I got the keys, I let Steve out and we made our **ESCAPE.**

I mean, it was a crazy plan. Like, could we save our world from the Infinity 2.0 Update?

THURSDAY

We spent a few days hiding at Steve's house while he tweaked the **TIME PORTAL.** No matter how many times it happened, I was still weirded out being woken up by Emma licking my face. If I had a spine, it would be shivering.

Anyway, Steve finally finished all the upgrades on the Time Portal. He even added a time dial to get us where we needed to go.

Turn it back!

'You ready to do this?' Steve asked me.

'I'm not... but we have to do this.'

Then Steve turned **THE DIAL** on the Time Portal and set it for us to travel a few months back, before the Infinity Update 2.0 was released.

Just as we were about to jump in...

PFFFZZT! BOOM!

Somebody fired **LASER BEAMS** at us!

'LOOK!' Steve yelled as he pointed down the street.

It was Mumma Mabel's robots in their robot spaceships, riding their robot Horses towards us and firing lasers at us.

'Dude, if we're gonna do this, we need to do this now!' Steve yelled.

Well, here goes nothing!

FFFZZZZZZZSSSH!

FRIDAY

FFFZZZZZZZSSSH!

We came out of the Time Portal **DETERMINED** to stop the Infinity 2.0 Update and get things back to normal.

Except when we got out of the Portal, it looked like Minecraft, just a little different.

'Wait a minute... where is everything?'

Never seen Minecraft so... plain

'I don't know,' Steve said. 'We might be in a new Biome?'

So we started walking around, hoping that we would eventually run into some trees. But no matter where we went, we saw **NOTHING.** We even started digging underground.

Still nothing.

'Dude, where did you bring us?'

Then I caught a glimpse of somebody really far away.

'Hey, look! There's some **BALD DUDE** with a goatee over there, let's go ask him.

So we ran over to where the guy was. Once the guy saw us, he started running away!

'AAAHHHHH! A Zombie and a guy with a weird-shaped head!' he yelled.

'Hey! Slow down,' I replied at him.
'We're not gonna hurt you, we
just need to know where we are!'

The guy turned around and slowly
walked over to us.

'Can you point us to Minecraft
MM Co. Towers?' I asked him.

'The what?'

'Minecraft MM Co. Towers... the
building with the big sign on top.'

'What's Minecraft?' the bald guy
asked.

Then I looked at Steve, who just shrugged.

'So where are we?' I asked the bald dude with the goatee.

'Oh, this is called **CAVE GAME.** I'm trying to design a first-player sandbox game, but I'm not sure what to do next.'

'Wait a minute... did you say, CAVE GAME?!'

'Yeah. I was thinking of calling it the "Order of the Stone" but it sounded kinda lame.'

'Uh... is your name **MARKUS?**'
I asked him, picking up my jaw
from the ground.

'Yeah, how'd you know? But please,
call me Notch,' the guy said
sticking his hand out to shake.

Not all heroes
wear capes

I couldn't wait to shake his hand...
but I checked for any mould sweat
on my palms first.

'You're Notch! Whoa! I'm your
biggest fan!'

'Really? I didn't even know I
had fans. Haven't really created
anything worth having fans for,
but cool... I dig it.'

'So, what update is this one?'
Steve asked.

'Update? If you mean what
version, I call it RD-132211.'

Then Steve grabbed my arm.
'Dude, I think we went all the
way back to **PRE-CLASSIC
MINECRAFT!**' he whispered.

'Seriously?!!'

'Yeah. And, I know you're excited,
but we got to get back to saving
the world.'

'Hey, can Notch help us?' I asked
Steve. 'Just tell him to stay true
to the game and not take the 2.5
billion dollar offer MM Co. make to
Mojang. I'm sure he'll do it.'

'No way! If we tell him anything,

it could change the future into something crazier than what it is now. Haven't you ever heard of the **BUTTERFLY EFFECT?'**

'Isn't that like when you leave your fly open and you don't really know about it until later, when you get home and your mum tells you? And then you realise you had it open all day... at school... and then you realise the cool kids weren't really laughing with you?'

'Uh, what?' Steve asked... giving me that cool eyebrow look.

'You know we could just tell Notch that his fly is open,' I said.

Steve just face-palmed really quick.

'Hey, Notch,' Steve said to Notch. 'Sorry, we got in your game. We accidentally logged onto your server, but we need to get back to finishing developing our game.'

'Oh, you guys are GAME DEVELOPERS too? What's the name of your game?'

'Roblux. Yeah, I'm still working on the name,' Steve said.

'Yeah... keep working on it. Names are always really lame when you start,' Notch said.

So, we said our good-byes and started heading back to the **TIME PORTAL.** But I had to try to convince Notch to help us, somehow.

I told Steve to hold up because I wanted to go back and ask Notch for his signature. As I was walking to Notch, I quickly wrote a note without Steve knowing.

'Here, Mr Notch,' I said. 'But don't

read it until the time is right.'

'Whoa, my first **FAN LETTER.**
Thanks, smelly green boy.'

I ran back to find Steve and
headed back to the Time Portal.

But when we got there, we got
the shock of our lives. There was a
huge chunk missing where the Time
Portal dial used to be!

'Man, no wonder it sent us all the
way back here!' Steve said. 'We
got hit by a robot's lasers.'

'So what do we do now?'

'Without that dial, if we jump in the Time Portal, we won't know where we'll end up,' Steve said. 'I could fix it, but there's nothing here to fix it with.'

Just as we were planning on what to do, suddenly we heard...

FFFZZZZZZZSSSH!

'There they are! Get them!' came an **ELECTRICAL VOICE.**

PFFFZZT! BOOM!

'It's the robots! We need to get out of here, Steve!' I shouted.

'But if we **JUMP IN** the Portal, we won't know where we'll end up,' Steve said.

'Dude, we don't have a choice. Anywhere is better than here!'

PFFFZZT! BOOM!

So, even though we had no idea where we would end up, we jumped head first into the Time Portal. At least we should be safe...

FFFZZZZZZZSSSH!

SATURDAY

FFFZZZZZZZSSSH!

'Dude, where are we now?' I said as I looked at Steve.

Except there was something wrong with Steve. He looked like Skelee except with a **BIGGER HEAD.**

Stelee, is that you?

'Steve, what's up with your skin?'

'Me? What happened to you? Why is your face all the way down near your belly button?'

'What the... ?'

Then we looked around and everything was **ALL WEIRD.**

There were Endermen with little legs, Withers with two heads, and there was this weird-looking thing trying to crawl up my leg...

Creeper Jockey?

'Dude! I think we actually
BROKE MINECRAFT!' I said.

'Whoa.'

Then I thought I saw a Villager
bobbing its head up and down
behind a bush.

'Hey, look, there's a Villager!' I
said. 'Let's ask him.'

But when we got to him, it wasn't

a normal Villager. It had his head on his shoulders, a head on his feet, and a head on his butt.

'What... is that?'

'I don't know, but it looks like it wants to talk to us,' Steve said.

'Yeah, what part?'

Then the weird Villager thing HOBBLED over to us.

'You folks new around here?' the creepy Villager said.

'Uh, yeah... hey, what Minecraft

update is this?'

'This is the greatest Minecraft Update that Mojang has ever made,' the two-headed Villager replied. **'MINECRAFT 1.7.10!** The ultimate Minecraft Update.'

'Ohhhhh! Now it makes sense,' I blurted. 'It sure explains all the craziness around here. Kinda explains why I can see through your head... and your clothes.'

'Seriously?' said Steve as he made a disgusted face.

'Hey, maybe we can find what we need to fix the Time Portal here?' I said. 'And if not, we can always make **A MOD** to do it.'

'Great idea,' Steve said.

But right before we were about to walk away and fix the Portal, we suddenly heard...

'HHOOLLLOOOLOOOOOAAAAA!!!!'

Next thing we know, a stick man with a huge square head ran towards us.

Like an extra skinny Skeleton

'You have returned! **THE PROPHECY** has come true!' the stick man said.

Then a group of other stick people came rushing over to us.

'Steve... I think you're the Chosen One,' I whispered to Steve.

'And now, we can start the **SACRIFICE!**' the weird stick

man yelled.

'HHOOLLLOOOLOOOOOAAAAA!!!!' cried the stick people mob.

'Uh... I don't what they're talking about,' Steve said. 'And that's our cue to GET OUT OF HERE!'

So we ran as fast as we could back to **THE PORTAL.**

'OH, SQUARE ONE! LET US FEAST ON YOUR CRANIUM FOR INFINITE KNOWLEDGE!' shouted the crowd.

This time, Steve and I didn't think

about where we were going, we jumped **HEAD-FIRST** into the Time Portal.

Oh, man, I really hope we don't die...

FFFZZZZZZZSSSH!

SUNDAY

FFFZZZZZZZSSSH!

'Uh Steve... something tells me we're not in Minecraft anymore.'

'Uh... what gave it away?' Steve said while getting a dollop of rainbow ice-cream that came out of a **UNICORN'S BUTT.**

'Yum, strawberry flavoured.'

'Dude, where are we?'

'I don't know,' Steve said.

Don't get me wrong. I liked the rainbow clouds, the lollipop trees and lake of chocolate milk. Not to mention the **CANDY CORN** fields were pretty cool. And cuddly teddy bears walking around was nice too.

🡅 What update is this?

'Oh no!' Steve said.

'What?'

'I'm gonna try something,' Steve said.

Then Steve yelled at the top of his voice...

'%$&*#@&%!'

Nothing. It was just silent. Steve looked really at a loss.

'Oh no! The child filter is on... like permanently!'

'Wait a minute... doesn't that mean?'

All of a sudden, a rainbow-coloured aeroplane flew by with a big sign at the end saying:

WELCOME TO MUM-CRAFT—
WHERE EVERY CHILD IS
SAFE FROM HARM.

And if that wasn't disturbing enough, all of a sudden, we heard...

ZZZZT... FZZZZLLL... BOOM!

We turned around to see where the **WEIRD SOUNDS** were coming from and our worst fears came true. Our Time Portal was dead.

After a few tears, we took a long
hard look out at everything.

'Is this what Minecraft is going
to turn into?' I asked him.

'Well, now that our Time Portal
is dead, we're **STUCK HERE**
forever. Minecraft "is" this now
the stupid...' sighed Steve and then
broke off. I figured the child filter
blocked sarcasm too.

Then a loud bell chimed a few
times and a song came on the
loudspeakers all over town.

Then a soothing voice came over

the loudspeaker and said, 'It's time for our **AFTERNOON NAP,** children. Cuddle your teddy, drink your warm milk, and pull up your warm blankie. Now ride the rainbow to dreamland.'

I tried very hard to resist the very soothing voice... but the teddy bears were so cuddly... and the blanket was so warm.

When I looked over at Steve, he was already falling fast asleep.

'Come on, man. We... can't... give... in...' I stuttered to Steve.

'Have beautiful dreams children and remember, Mum-Craft... where every child is safe from harm.'

ZZZZZZZZZ.

MONDAY

'Uuurrrggghhh!' I yawned as I woke up in the arms of a giant teddy.

After the grogginess of sleep left me, I realised how weird all this was. I jumped up.

'DUDE! WAKE UP!' shaking Steve awake.

'Five more minutes... I don't wanna get up.'

'Dude, we need to get out of here!' I **SHOOK** Steve until he realised where we were... not in the Minecraft we know.

Steve jumped up and we both ran out of there.

'Can't you find something here to fix the Time Portal?' I asked Steve as we ran away.

'What's the use? We don't know where to go... and even if we know, how do we even get there? We might as well just accept it... it's over.'

I couldn't believe what I was hearing. I would clean my ear wax, but I might need it for a **SNACK** later. Steve was giving up? Steve never gives up.

Then Steve sat down on the warm blanket covered hills, cuddled up into a ball, and started to sleep.

'STEVE!'

'Seriously, man, what's the use?' he said.

'Dude, we owe it to the people we know. We owe it to all the millions of kids who didn't have a life before Minecraft. Remember how bad those days were?'

'Yeah.'

'And remember when kids spent hours trying to figure out how to make servers? And when they finally figured it out, how they were able to make friends from all around the world? And nerdy kids became cool and **MINECRAFT MEMES** became a thing?'

'Yeah.'

'Bro, are we really going to give up? Or are we going to stand up for the millions of Minecraft obsessed kids around the world? And are we going to fight for all the **MINECON FANS** that braved punishment for skipping school so they could be a part of the most amazing event ever?'

'YEAH! Let's do this!' shouted Steve.

Yup, the Chosen One was back!

We spent the afternoon fixing the Time Portal with licorice sticks, candy corn, and strawberry syrup.

'I think it's only going to hold up for one more trip,' Steve said as he placed the final knob on the Time Portal. 'So, this trip is the last. There's no going home.'

'That's fine by me, bro,' I replied with determination.

Steve got ready to turn the time dial made out of a **ZOREO COOKIE.** We just had to pick where we were going to go.

'How about we go to the greatest Minecraft Update ever?' Steve asked me.

I just gave him a really big,

CHEESY, YELLOW SMILE

and said 'Minecraft Update 1.8!'

Here we come!

FFFZZZZZZZZSSSH!

TUESDAY

FFFZZZZZZZSSSH!

We made it. Minecraft Update 1.8!

Ahh. I could smell the adventure
in the air.

ZZZZT... FZZZZLLL... BRRRTTTT...
BOOM!

And that was the Time Portal.
There was no going back. This was
our **NEW HOME** now.

Anyway, today just happened

to be the day that Mojang
makes the deal with MM Co.
and the beginning of the end for
Minecraft.

So we went back to Steve's house
to grab some **SUPPLIES.** You
know, smoke bombs, grappling
hooks, the usual heist items.

So once we were all ready, we
trekked to MM Co. Towers for our
final showdown.

We finally made it to MM Co.
Towers, and we hid in the hills
overlooking the building.

↖ The perfect villain hideout!

The place was guarded with
like a hundred security guards.
MUMMA MABEL had plotted
this takeover for years. She
didn't want anything, or anybody,
stopping her from taking over
Minecraft.

'So, what's our plan, Steve?'

'Well, we need to get into MM Co. Towers and stop Notch from selling Mojang... I think I have a plan to take care of the hundreds of security guards,' Steve replied with a big, cheesy smile.

Then, we walked to the **ELECTRIC CONTROL** panel outside.

'Here, put these in your ears,' Steve said, handing me candy corns.

'What are these for?'

'You'll see,' Steve said as he pulled

out a huge radio from his backpack.

I had enough ear wax... but I didn't have time to tell Steve. So I plugged them into my ear holes.

Then Steve opened the control panel and wired the radio to some Redstone switches that connected to the sound system.

'Well, here goes nothing,' he said.

Then he pressed **PLAY.**

'It's time for our afternoon nap, children. Cuddle your teddy, drink your warm milk, and pull up your warm blankie. Now ride the rainbow to dreamland,' announced the **HYPNOTIC VOICE** around the building.

Suddenly, the guards at the front started dropping like flies.

'Have beautiful dreams children and remember, Mum-Craft... where every child is safe from harm.'

When the last guard finally fell asleep, Steve and I made our move. We grabbed a keycard from a sleeping guard and made it into the building.

At the lobby, we looked at the office map and read: CEO-Mabel Mumbottom—Top Floor.

Of course, all the elevators were shut down, so we had to take the stairs to the top floor... all **87 FLOORS** of them.

Yeah, remember I told you I run like a one-hundred-year-old man? After a few hours, I looked like a one-hundred-year-old man who got stuck in a tanning booth... for about a week... then exploded.

But there it was, the CEO's office

was right in front of us.

'This is it, man! I'll rush in and create **A DISTRACTION** and you grab Notch and throw him out the window.'

'Seriously?!!' I huffed.

'Nah, just kidding. I'll create a distraction and you sneak Notch out before they know what hit them. Deal?' Steve asked.

'Deal!'

✳ TUESDAY
LATER THAT DAY

BAM!!!!!

Steve burst in through the doors and threw a few smoke bomb potions in the room.

BOOOSSHHH!

COUGH! COUGH!

Everybody was coughing, but it didn't bother me... I don't have lungs, remember?

Anyway, I looked around through

the room to see if I could see Notch's bald head. But a robot transformed into a huge fan and blew the smoke out of the room.

And once the smoke cleared, Steve was in the grip of one of Mumma Mabel's robot minions with Mabel standing there with her **SMUG MUM** face.

'MUAHAHAHAHA!,' Mabel laughed... in what felt like surround sound.

I turned around and there were two Mumma Mabels!

'I had a feeling you'd be coming

here,' one of the Mabels said, 'so I came to **WARN MYSELF** and prevent you from screwing up our deal to buy Mojang.'

Anyway, then both future and present Mabel started cackling, 'MMUUAAHHAAHHAAHHAAHHAA!'

Man, this time travel stuff is really giving me a headache. I was hitting my pea brain to get rid of the pain when a robot jumped me from behind and grabbed me.

'Take them to my Time Portal,' future Mabel said. 'Send them back to where they won't cause any trouble. I think a nice visit to the Sheepinator should cure them of their trouble making once and for all. MUAHAHAHAHA!'

Then, as they were dragging us away, Notch and his lawyers came out of the closet. This was my **LAST CHANCE!**

'Notch, don't do it, man! Don't sell out! Stay true to the game, man!!!'

But from the shame on Notch's face with the pen in his hand, I could tell we were too late.

The robots took us downstairs where Mabel's Time Portal was waiting. I looked over to Steve, and he gave me a look of pride.

And even though we failed, he still gave me a **THUMBS-UP.**

And I gave one back.

Then they threw us into the Time Portal.

FFFZZZZZZZSSSH!

WEDNESDAY

FFFZZZZZZZSSSH!

We thought we would have a painful **ROBOT WELCOME,** but we were back at Steve's house.

'Hey, where is everybody?' I asked Steve. 'And why are we back at your house?'

'I don't know. But, honestly, I'm too tired to care right now.'

I could tell Steve was sad. I

Couldn't blame him... I mean, **WE FAILED.**

And now Minecraft would never be the same awesome game loved by kids all over the world, ever again.

I got really sad too.

So we just laid there and cried ourselves to sleep.

THURSDAY

I was expecting to be woken up by a rainbow Sheep licking my face. But instead, I heard...

'BREAKFAST!'

'Uuuurrgghhwhazzzzat?'

'Hey, Steve... Zombie, come in here and get breakfast before it gets cold,' somebody yelled.

'**WAIT...** how do Sheep know how to make breakfast?' I asked Steve.

Steve was as weirded out as I was.

So we got up and slowly walked in to his house, and we were totally **BLOWN AWAY.**

'OWEN!' Steve and I shouted.

Normal, Villager Owen was at the table! And then a Villager lady walked into the kitchen.

'EMMA!' we cried.

'You guys are back!' Steve yelled as he gave them both hugs and pinched their long noses.

'Uh... I think you'd better stop punching those trees,' Owen said, a little creeped out. 'I think it's causing more damage than the doctor said it would.'

Steve and I ran outside after breakfast to celebrate!

'Dude, **WE DID IT!** Somehow, we did it!' Steve sang.

'But how?' I asked. 'I saw Notch with the pen in his hand. I was sure he sold Mojang to MM Co.'

Then Old Man Jenkins walked by with his Zombie horse. We were so happy to see him and both **TACKLED** him with hugs.

'What in tarnation has gotten in to you two?!! It's bad enough that I have to put up with all these new Minecraft updates. Now you fellas start acting all squirrely.'

'New updates? What new updates?' Steve asked.

Then he pulled out his Redstone phone with his left hand, and with his right hand he started pushing buttons.

'Dude, look!' I said to Steve. 'Dual

wielding!'

Then we tackled Old Man Jenkins again out of joy.

After we helped him put himself back together, he looked at his phone and said, 'Well, right now we are on **MINECRAFT 1.12**. That's what it says on the MM Co. website.'

'Wait... MM Co.! You mean MM Co. still bought Mojang?!!' I gasped.

'Have you boys been glitching or something? Of course, MM Co. bought Mojang. Happened a few years ago.' Old Man Jenkins sighed then took off before we could tackle him again.

'So, Steve, what happened? If MM Co. still bought Mojang, then why is everything still the same?'

'I don't know, Dude. I don't know.'

'Hey, where you guys been?' A voice called from behind me.

It was **SKELEE!**

'Yeah, we haven't seen you guys since yesterday,' somebody said.

It was Slimey!

'Yeah, you guys went outside to go play with your new Time Portal and then you just disappeared.'

It was Creepy!

'Oh, man! Am I glad to see you guys,' I said.

'Yeah, we thought you guys were gone for good,' Steve said.

The guys just gave us a **WEIRD LOOK...** but we tackled them anyway.

THURSDAY
LATER THAT DAY

So we started telling the guys the story of our excellent adventure, when suddenly...

FFFZZZZZZZSSSH!

A Time Portal appeared and robots started coming through!

FFFZZZZZZZSSSH!

There was like a **WHOLE ARMY** of them.

And last but not least...

FFFZZZZZZZSSSH!

'MUAHAHAHAHA! Did you think you could escape from me?'

It was **MUMMA MABEL!**

'Face it, Mabel!' I said. 'You lost! And now Minecraft is back to the way it should be!'

'Oh, you think you are so smart? Because you managed to convince Notch to put a clause in his contract that said he would only sell Minecraft if they fired me as the CEO... ' Mabel screeched as her robot army got into battle formation.

Then the robots started shifting...

'Just because you **DESTROYED MY 30 YEARS** of hard work...'

And then the robots combined...

'That doesn't mean I can't still destroy you!'

Then Mumma Mabel jumped into the middle of the pile of robots and they all started to transform!

TSCHE-CHU-CHU-CHE-CHE-TSCHE!

'So get ready to be destroyed by...
the **TER-MUM-INATOR!**'

I couldn't believe my eyes. Mabel
had a huge metalloid robot body
and these giant, long probes for
hands. It's like Craftformers
escaped our TV screens!

CHUK, CHAK!

'ARE YOU READY FOR ME TO
TAKE YOUR TEMPERATURE?'
asked the robot.

'**RUN!**' shouted Steve.

PFFFZZT! BOOM!

The guys and I all scattered
before she could blast us into next
week... maybe even next year.

'It's not over yet!' Mumma Mabel
yelled. 'After I destroy you, I'll
go back through the Time Portal
and make Notch sign over all of
Minecraft to me! MUAHAHA!'

PFFFZZT! BOOM!

We all hid behind some trees near
Steve's house.

'Hey, what are we going to do?
She's too powerful,' Skelee said.

'We have to **DESTROY** her Time Portal or we'll be eating grass every day,' Steve said.

'I'm scared, Zombie,' Creepy said. 'HSSSSSS.'

I looked over at Steve's garage and a small glimmer caught the corner of my eye socket.

'Oh, yeah, I think all of us will totally be enough!' I said pointing to Steve's garage.

We all looked at each other, and we all knew what we had to do.

Steve threw a **SMOKE BOMB** potion to create a diversion.

Then when Mumma Mabel wasn't looking, we all ran and dived head first into Steve's garage...

FFFZZZZZZZSSSH!

THURSDAY
EVEN LATER THAT DAY

PFFFZZT! BOOM!

'Where are you? You little wretched mobs?!!!' Mumma Mabel yelled.

PFFFZZT! BOOM!

'You can hide as long as you like, because I am going to eventually get rid of all of you **HOSTILE MOBS** and Minecraft will be mine once and for all!'

PFFFZZT! BOOM!

'Well Mabel, what you have totally underestimated about Minecraft mobs... is that there is more to us than meets the eye!'

THUMP! THUMP!

AUTO-MOBS, ATTACK!

'NOW, STEVE... FIST PUNCH!'

'HYAAAAAAAAHHHHHHH!!!!!!'

BBBBBBOOOOOOOMMMMMM!

Mabel didn't know what hit her. I felt bad punching someone in the face... but I think Mabel totally deserved it.

'Hey, guys, she's getting up!'

'NOW, SLIMEY... SUPER JUMP **BODY SLAM!**'

KABOOM!

'Man, that should've put her down,

but she's still getting up!'

'SKELEE... BOW AND ARROW,
NOW!' shouted Steve.

THWIP!

Aim and fire!

KRESH!

FZZZZTTT, BBRRRRTT, BOOM!

'Yeah, that did it. It totally fried her circuits!'

'NOW, CREEPY... FINISHING TOUCH... DROP THE BOMB!'

HSSSSSSS...
PPPPFFFFFFFRRRRTTTTT

'**EWWWWW!**' gasped Mumma Mabel and then she crashed.

'We did it!' shouted Creepy.

We started jumping up and down, celebrating. But then we heard the police sirens.

We jumped back into Steve's Portal and turned back to normal.

We came out to find that it wasn't the regular police, it was the **CYBER POLICE** that surrounded us.

'ALL RIGHT, EVERYBODY, STAY WHERE YOU ARE!' somebody with a megaphone shouted.

We just stood there frozen with our hands up. We watched as a black van pulled up and the front door opened.

'You guys can put your hands

down now,' a guy in a fedora said.

'Hey, look, it's Notch!' Steve yelled.

We were so happy, we just tackled him with hugs.

'All right, you guys. It's good to see you too,' smiled Notch.

'But I thought you **SOLD OUT** to MM Co.?' I asked Notch. 'So what happened?

'Well, I was about to sign my baby over to MM Co. But, when I saw them take you away, I remembered your letter.'

'What letter?' Steve asked.

'**OH NOTHING...**' I said. 'Go on, Notch.'

'Well, I couldn't give up my baby that easily, so not only did I make sure they fired Mabel, I created the Cyber Police to make sure nobody ever messed with Minecraft ever again.'

We were so happy to hear that, that we tackled Notch again.

'Oh, there's one more change I made,' Notch said looking at me. 'Hey, Zombie, you want a job? There's a Mob Game Coder internship that I think you'd be perfect for.'

'Me... seriously?!!' I shouted.

Whoa! It was the best news I had ever heard. My dream was finally coming true!

'What about me?' Steve asked. 'I am the CHOSEN ONE after all.'

'Well, you just stick with your Roblux game,' Notch said with a smile. 'Just keep working on that name.'

'So what are you going to do with Mumma Mabel?' Steve asked.

'Well, I think she's going to have plenty of time to think about what she did after a nice, long and **VERY HOT STAY** in the Nether Fortress.'

'Nice!' the guys and I replied.

SUNDAY
A FEW DAYS LATER

Well, Minecraft is **BACK TO NORMAL** again.

Not only is Minecraft better than ever, I start an internship to become a game developer tomorrow. Who knows... maybe I'll be part of the team that releases the next Minecraft update.

Anyway, Steve and I are done with time travelling. Forever. The Cyber Police took away our Time

Portal and Mumma Mabel's too.

But the Cyber Police did let us keep the Craftformer Portal. They said it means they can call us in if there was another cataclysmic world-ending event.

The guys and I did combine a few more times... it made our CRAFTFORMER games so much more fun.

But it got kind of weird when we started to become too much like each other.

I mean, I got really tired of

smelling my own farts.

But Steve and Skelee still use it to play **PRANKS** on Villagers, though.

Gotcha!

Mumma Mabel is still in Nether Fortress. They got her scooping **GHAST POOP** most of the time, which serves her right.

But, I think I might go visit her soon. She did just want to make Minecraft safe for kids, which was pretty cool.

Even though she was mean about it... I'm sure she's not that bad deep down.

Like deep, deep, deep, deep down.

But you know what I really learned from my excellent

adventure? That instead of worrying about the mistakes you made in the past, think about how you can learn from them to become a better mob.

And, I learned that you can sell your gaming company for a kazillion dollars and still not be a sell-out.

So tomorrow, I start my internship to be a **GAME DEVELOPER.** Maybe I'll come out with the next awesome game that changes the world.

Or at least makes it a better place for kids everywhere... and makes a **KAZILLION DOLLARS.**

But however it turns out, I know it's going to be... most excellent!

DIARY OF A MINECRAFT ZOMBIE

Have you ever wondered
what life is like for a
Minecraft Zombie?

COLLECT THEM ALL!

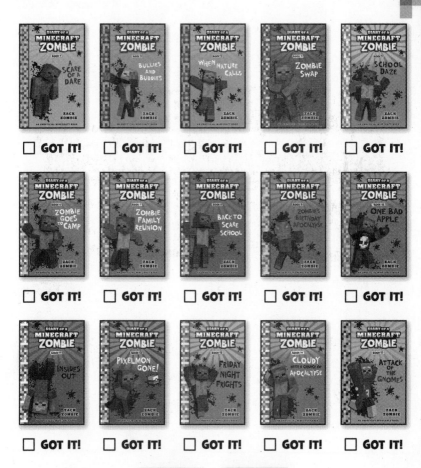

DIARY OF A MINECRAFT ZOMBIE — BOOK 1 — A SCARE OF A DARE	DIARY OF A MINECRAFT ZOMBIE — BOOK 2 — BULLIES AND BUDDIES	DIARY OF A MINECRAFT ZOMBIE — BOOK 3 — WHEN NATURE CALLS	DIARY OF A MINECRAFT ZOMBIE — BOOK 4 — ZOMBIE SWAP	DIARY OF A MINECRAFT ZOMBIE — BOOK 5 — SCHOOL DAZE
☐ **GOT IT!**	☐ **GOT IT!**	☐ **GOT IT!**	☐ **GOT IT!**	☐ **GOT IT!**
DIARY OF A MINECRAFT ZOMBIE — BOOK 6 — ZOMBIE GOES TO CAMP	DIARY OF A MINECRAFT ZOMBIE — BOOK 7 — ZOMBIE FAMILY REUNION	DIARY OF A MINECRAFT ZOMBIE — BOOK 8 — BACK TO SCARE SCHOOL	DIARY OF A MINECRAFT ZOMBIE — BOOK 9 — ZOMBIE'S BIRTHDAY APOCALYPSE	DIARY OF A MINECRAFT ZOMBIE — BOOK 10 — ONE BAD APPLE
☐ **GOT IT!**	☐ **GOT IT!**	☐ **GOT IT!**	☐ **GOT IT!**	☐ **GOT IT!**
DIARY OF A MINECRAFT ZOMBIE — BOOK 11 — INSIDES OUT	DIARY OF A MINECRAFT ZOMBIE — BOOK 12 — PIXELMON GONE!	DIARY OF A MINECRAFT ZOMBIE — BOOK 13 — FRIDAY NIGHT FRIGHTS	DIARY OF A MINECRAFT ZOMBIE — BOOK 14 — CLOUDY WITH A CHANCE OF APOCALYPSE	DIARY OF A MINECRAFT ZOMBIE — BOOK 15 — ATTACK OF THE GNOMES
☐ **GOT IT!**	☐ **GOT IT!**	☐ **GOT IT!**	☐ **GOT IT!**	☐ **GOT IT!**

DIARY OF A MINECRAFT ZOMBIE — BOOK 16 — DOWN THE DRAIN

DIARY OF A MINECRAFT ZOMBIE — BOOK 17 — ZOMBIE'S EXCELLENT ADVENTURE

☐ **GOT IT!**   ☑ **GOT IT!**

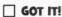

FIND OUT
WHAT HAPPENS
NEXT!

Zombie and his **friends** must visit the Ocean monument to stop the world of Minecraft from being

PLUNGED INTO THE DEPTHS OF THE SEA!

CAN ZOMBIE SAVE MINECRAFT FROM A WATERY GRAVE?